Judy Delton

BRIMHALL Comes to Stay

illustrations by Cyndy Szekeres

Lothrop, Lee & Shepard Company
A Division of William Morrow & Company, Inc.
New York

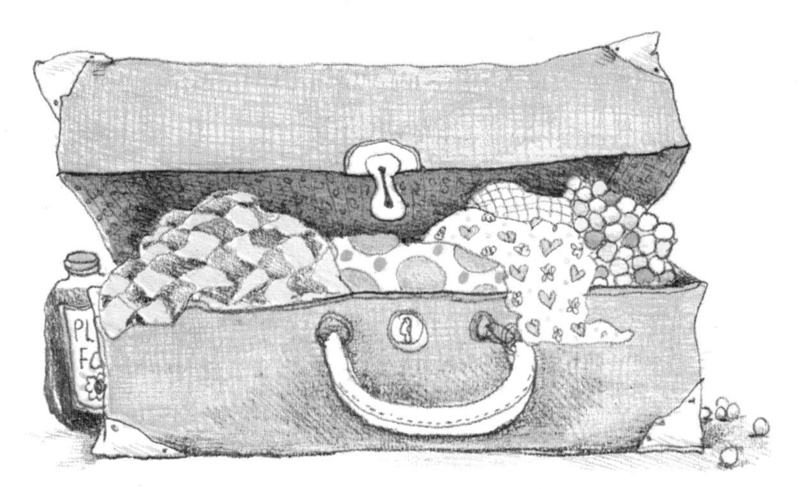

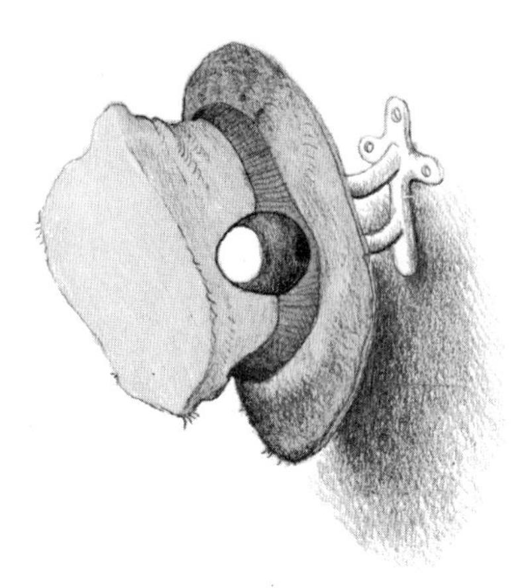

For Jina Marie Delton, who allows, celebrates, and nourishes the child in me.

Library of Congress Cataloging in Publication Data
Delton, Judy.
Brimhall comes to stay.
SUMMARY: Bear welcomes the arrival of his cousin Brimhall to live with him, but Brimhall's eccentric habits soon tax Bear's hospitality.
[1. Bears—Fiction. 2. Family life—Fiction] I. Szekeres, Cindy. II. Title.
PZ7.D388Br [E] 78-7524
ISBN 0-688-41863-5
ISBN 0-688-51863-X lib. bdg.

Printed in the United States of America.

First Edition
1 2 3 4 5 6 7 8 9 10

CONTENTS

1

BEAR'S NEWS

"Raccoon!" called Bear, racing
up the path to Raccoon's house.
"Are you home, Raccoon?"
Bear knocked on Raccoon's door.
Raccoon opened it.
"Hello," he said. "Why, Bear,
you are all out of breath!"
Bear waved an envelope at
Raccoon and sat down to rest
on the doorstep.

"I ran all the way, Raccoon. This letter just came from my cousin Brimhall. I have news!"

"Brimhall?" said Raccoon, sitting down beside Bear. "Is he the same Brimhall who made teacups out of wax, and then tried to sell them?"

Bear nodded. "His teacups were just fine, Raccoon. But the customers' tea was much too hot. The cups melted, and—"

"What does Brimhall say in his letter, Bear?" asked Raccoon, changing the subject.

"He is coming here, Raccoon!
Brimhall is coming to live
with me! He says he has
'outgrown' his apartment."
Bear looked at the letter in
his paw. "And he says that he
needs more 'exposure.' "
"Exposure?" said Raccoon. "What
does he mean by that, Bear?"
Bear scratched his head.

"He probably wants to meet new friends," said Bear kindly. "I am so excited, Raccoon! It is easier to cook for two, you know. And Brimhall is a fine chess player."

Raccoon looked relieved. He didn't like to play chess.

"Why, that is very good news, Bear!" said Raccoon. "When does Brimhall arrive?"

"Any day, Raccoon. Any day now." Bear's eyes grew bright.

"I must get home and bake," said Bear, standing up. "Huckleberry pie, that's Brimhall's favorite."

Raccoon got up, too.

"I'm glad to hear your news, Bear," he said. "I'm looking forward to meeting your cousin."

2

BRIMHALL ARRIVES

Bear said good-bye and walked home, humming to himself. As he came around a pine tree, he saw someone with a suitcase in one paw and a piece of paper in the other. He was looking at the number on Bear's front door.

"Brimhall!" Bear called. "Is that you?"

"Why, Bear! This is the right house! I asked directions at Three Oaks." Brimhall hugged Bear. "You haven't changed a bit, Bear."

Bear threw his paws around Brimhall. "Welcome, Brimhall. I am so glad you are here!"

Bear took Brimhall's suitcase, and opened the door.

"What a fine house!" said Brimhall. "A fine house, Bear. Splendid southern exposure."

"Here is your room, Brimhall," said Bear, setting the suitcase

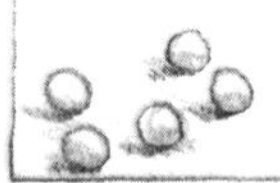

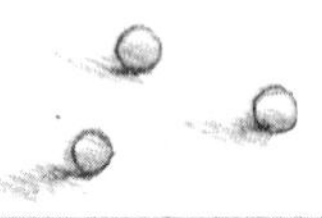

on the bed. "Is this all you brought with you?"

"The van comes tomorrow," said Brimhall.

He opened his suitcase.

Out spilled dozens of small, white balls.

They rolled under the bed and out the door.

"Er—what are those?" Bear said, as he and Brimhall scrambled after them.

"Mothballs," said Brimhall, "—don't you keep them on hand?"

"No," said Bear. "Should I?"

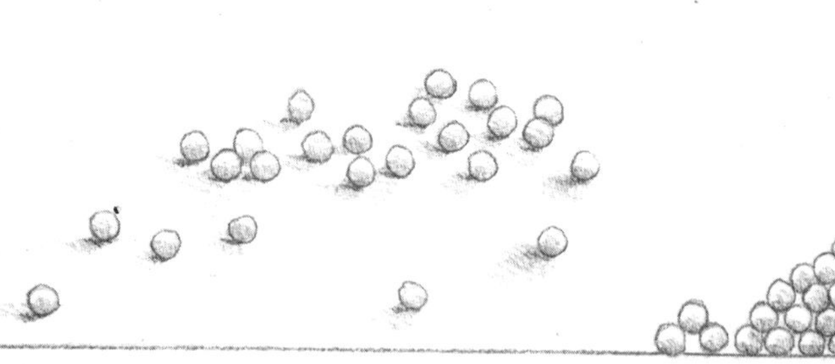

"Certainly," said Brimhall, straightening his vest. "Moths eat holes in clothes, you know. Mothballs keep moths away. Look at my suit, Bear. Do you see a hole in it?"

Brimhall held up his suit.

More mothballs rolled out.

"I have never had a hole in my suit, Brimhall," said Bear.

"Lucky," said Brimhall, hanging his suit in the closet. "I came just in time, then."

While Brimhall made himself at home, Bear went to the kitchen.

He got out his flour and butter.
He washed his huckleberries.
Soon his pie was in the oven.
While the pie baked, Bear made dinner.

"My," said Brimhall, sniffing the air as he came into the kitchen. "You are as good a cook as ever, Bear. Huckleberry pie?"

Bear nodded, and took a deep
sniff himself.
All he could smell was mothballs.
Brimhall leaned over the stove
to stir the gravy.
Three mothballs rolled out of
his vest pocket and into the pan.
"My goodness," said Bear.
He removed them with a spoon.
The cousins had a fine dinner.
They talked about good times
they had shared.

Brimhall told Bear about Aunt Beryl and Uncle Berman, who were traveling in Alaska.

Bear served the huckleberry pie. After his fifth piece, Brimhall leaned back and put his feet up on the table.

"Bear," he said, juggling seven mothballs, "you are a fine cousin. I am so glad I have come to stay with you."

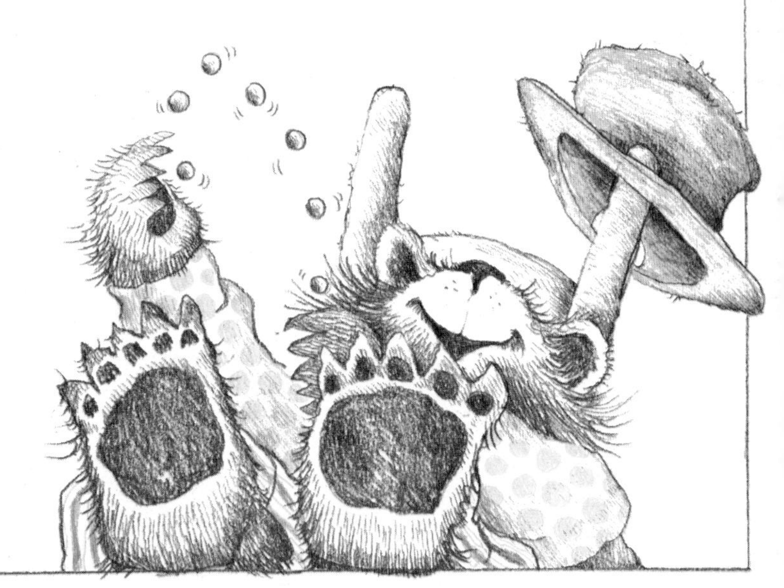

"It is wonderful to have you,
Brimhall," said Bear, clearing
the table. "The spare bedroom
is just right for you. And it's
far easier to cook for two,
you know."
Brimhall helped Bear wash the
dishes.

Before bed they played two games of chess.

They each won a game.

"My, it is fine to have a chess partner!" said Bear.

"It's good I'm here," Brimhall said, folding the chessboard, "I came just in time. Now I think I'll turn in, Bear."

"Goodnight, Brimhall," said Bear.

Bear took a bath and brushed his teeth.

He hummed as he put on his pajamas.

It was good to have someone in the spare bedroom.
Bear turned off the light and climbed into bed.
As he drifted off to sleep, he heard a strange rasping noise.
It sounded as if someone were sawing wood.
"What could that be?" Bear mumbled. "I must be dreaming."
He turned over and fell asleep.

3

BRIMHALL GETS SETTLED

The next morning, Bear was up early.

He tiptoed past Brimhall's door and into the kitchen.

There he made cocoa, and sat down at the table to read the morning paper.

"Why," said Bear, "I must have grown overnight. My legs don't fit under my own table!"

Bear looked at the tabletop.
It seemed closer to the floor
than it had been yesterday.
Bear got down and peered under
the table.
There was sawdust on the floor.
"Someone has sawed off the
table legs!" Bear said. "Now
who would do that?"
The smell of mothballs wafted
into the kitchen.
Brimhall padded in.
"Good morning, Bear," he said,
pouring a cup of cocoa.

"Good morning, Brimhall," said
Bear. "Did you sleep well?"

"Fine, fine," said Brimhall,
"—that is, when I got the bed
raised high enough."

"High enough?" said Bear.

"Yes, Bear," said Brimhall, "I am a big bear, you know."

"Why, so am I," said Bear, "but I have no trouble getting into my bed. It's the same height as yours."

"Not into," said Brimhall, patiently, "under."

"UNDER?" said Bear.

Brimhall dropped three marshmallows into his cocoa.

He took out one mothball.

"Brimhall," Bear said, "no one sleeps under the bed."

"I do," said Brimhall.

Bear looked at his table.

Then he went into Brimhall's

room and looked at the bed.

"Brimhall," he called, "are these my table legs on your bed?"

"Why, yes," said Brimhall, taking a sip of his cocoa.

"Oh, dear," said Bear.

"Don't feel bad, Bear. It wasn't your fault the bed was too low," said Brimhall kindly. "It's just right, now."

"Brimhall, your bed may be high enough, but now my table is much too low!" said Bear.

"Not if you sit on the floor, Bear," said Brimhall. "See? It's very comfortable."

Bear looked doubtful.

"Just try it," said Brimhall.

Bear sat down carefully and
folded his legs like Brimhall.
Brimhall poured Bear another
cup of cocoa.
Then he made Bear a piece of
cinnamon toast.
"Why, thank you, Brimhall," said
Bear. "I suppose I could get
used to sitting on the floor."

"Good," said Brimhall. "We'll need the chairs to put plants on."

"Plants?" said Bear.

Just then there was knock on the door.

"Mr. Brimhall? Sign here," said someone in a gray uniform.

"My plants have arrived," said Brimhall, signing. "This way."

The movers carried in a large palm tree.

"Over here, by the south window," Brimhall said. "Palm trees need all the sun they can get."

"Where to with these?" called the movers from the door.

"Ferns need a north window. Bear, can you help me with this?"

"Where are you taking my sofa,
Brimhall? I liked it there,"
said Bear.

"Then you'll like it even better
over here," said Brimhall.
Finally, the movers had moved
everything in.

There were plants on the sofa
and on the bookcase.
There were plants on the stove
and on top of the toaster.
Where Bear's flour jar had been
sat an African violet.
On his honey pot was some ivy.
"Now it looks like home," said
Brimhall.
"Now it looks like a jungle,"

said Bear in a muffled voice.

"What's that, Bear?" Brimhall said, as he watered his rubber tree. "My, this got dry on the trip. But wasn't it lucky they all got here safely?"

Bear sneezed. "Yes, Brimhall. It was very lucky. They all look quite healthy."

Bear sneezed again.

"I must be getting a cold," said Bear.

BEAR IS CURED

The next day, Bear baked with
plants on his stove.
The cousins sat on the floor
to eat.
They played chess with plants
on the chessboard.
On Wednesday, Bear's back ached.
"It must be from bending over
this low table to roll out my
piecrust," Bear said to himself.

Bear went to get his hot water bottle.
It was not in the closet and not in the drawer.
"Brimhall," Bear said at last, "have you seen my hot water bottle?"
"Why, yes, Bear," said Brimhall, "I am using it to warm my fig tree."
"Oh, dear, Brimhall, my back is aching. I am afraid I need it."
Bear sneezed.
"My goodness, I think you are coming down with something, Bear.

Get right to bed. I have just
the cure for you."
Brimhall bundled Bear into bed.
He put the hot water bottle
under him, and three comforters
on top of him.

"I'll be right back," Brimhall said. "Don't move, Bear."

"How can I?" said Bear weakly from under the comforters.

Brimhall returned with a jar.

"Now I'll just rub some of this on your chest, Bear, and you'll be well in no time."

Brimhall covered Bear's chest
with a sticky white ointment.
"This is made from the bark of a
rare Asian tree," Brimhall said.
"Brimhall, it is sticky, and it
smells very strong," said Bear.
"The stronger, the better,"
said Brimhall. "This can cure
almost anything."
Bear sighed.
"Now," said Brimhall, "I will
bring you some sassafras tea.

You will be well in no time."
Brimhall brought in a steaming
teapot and poured Bear a cup.
Bear took a sip and spluttered.
He took another sip, and coughed.
"Brimhall, this tastes terrible,"
said Bear, pushing the cup away
with a sticky paw.
"It takes getting used to," said
Brimhall kindly. "And now I'll
just set up the chessboard.
Maybe later you'll feel like a game."
Brimhall put the chessboard
on a stool beside Bear's bed.

Then he sat down in Bear's
rocking chair.
"I'll be right here if you need
anything, Bear."
Brimhall folded his paws in his
lap and rocked and hummed.
Soon he was asleep.

Bear felt the hot water bottle
too hot under his back.
He smelled Brimhall's sticky
ointment on his chest.
He tasted the bitter taste of
Brimhall's tea in his mouth.
He listened to Brimhall snore
beside the bed.
"Brimhall means well," thought
Bear, "but this is too much."

Bear got up and took a bath.
Then he went to the kitchen and
started some stew for dinner.
When Brimhall awoke, he looked
around for Bear.
He smelled the stew and came
into the kitchen.
"I see I cured you, Bear!" said
Brimhall. "I knew you would be
well in no time! Well, I must
go to Three Oaks now and get
some plant food. If you don't
need me, Bear, that is."
"Fine," said Bear. "Take your
time, Brimhall."

5

BEAR'S DECISION

After Brimhall had gone, there was a knock on the door.

"Come in," called Bear.

"Hello, Bear," said Raccoon and Porcupine, "we came to meet Brimhall. Is he settled now?"

"Oh, yes, Brimhall is settled," said Bear. "He is not at home right now. Do sit down."

"Where?" asked Raccoon.

"Er—why, here," said Bear, removing two plants from the sofa. "Brimhall collects plants."

"Yes, I see," said Raccoon.

"What is that unusual smell, Bear?" asked Porcupine.

"Stew," said Bear quickly.

Raccoon and Porcupine sniffed.

"No, Bear, it doesn't smell like stew—"

"Then it must be Brimhall's mothballs," Bear sighed. "He collects those, too. But I do have hot stew on the stove.

Would you care for some?"
"Why, that sounds good," said
Raccoon and Porcupine.
Bear filled two dishes with
stew and brought them into
the living room.

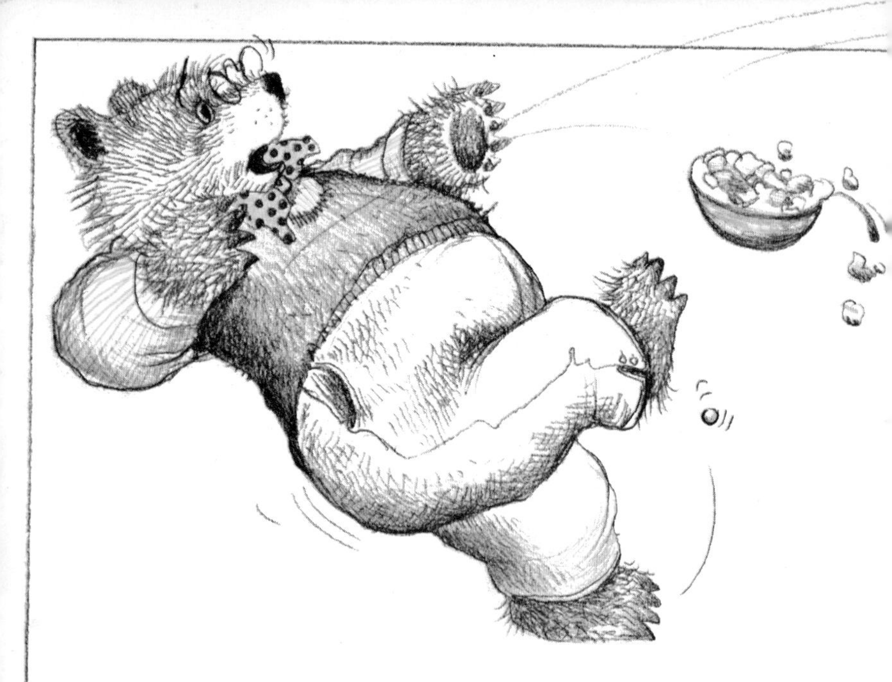

Suddenly, his feet slid out
from under him.
The two dishes of stew flew
into an avocado tree.
"A mothball! I slipped on a
MOTHBALL!" cried Bear.
Raccoon and Porcupine helped
him to his feet.
"That does it!" said Bear.

"Brimhall must go! My back aches from bending over a table that is too low. All I smell is mothballs, all day long. And as for these plants"—Bear sneezed—"it's like a jungle in here."

"Why, it's like bringing the outside in, Bear," Raccoon said. "I rather like it."

"And the mothballs smell clean, Bear," added Porcupine.

"Clean or not," said Bear, "Brimhall is driving me crazy. He simply has to go."

Bear sneezed again.

Raccoon looked at the plants.

Then he looked at Bear.

"Do you have an allergy, Bear?

My nephew has allergies. He

can't have plants in the house."

"That settles it!" said Bear.

"I will tell Brimhall as soon as he comes home. And as for his plants, I will get rid of them right now!"

"Now take it easy, Bear," said Raccoon. "Think this over. After all, Brimhall is family."

"Family or not," shouted Bear,
"enough is enough!"

Bear seized a cactus and carried it out the door.

"Let's come back later, Raccoon," whispered Porcupine.

Bear took all the plants outside. Then he swept the floor, and threw away all the mothballs.

Bear looked at his kitchen table. He went to the bookcase and took out eight thick books. He put two under each table leg.

Then Bear moved his sofa back where it belonged.

He sat down to rest.
"There!" he said, "that is much better. I don't smell mothballs any more. And I seem to have stopped sneezing."

6
COMPANY FOR DINNER

Just then the door opened and
in walked Brimhall, whistling.
"Hello, Bear!" he called. "Have
you had dinner yet?"
"No, Brimhall, no I haven't."
"That's good," said Brimhall,
"because I brought—"
Bear took a deep breath.
"Brimhall, I have decided there
must be some changes around here."

Brimhall looked around.

"Why, Bear, you put the plants outside. What a good idea. Now we have room to move in here."

"I threw out all the mothballs," Bear went on.

"Good idea, Bear. I haven't seen a moth since I came. Now let me tell you about dinner."

There was a tap on the door.

"Oh, my!" said Bear, "I forgot about Raccoon and Porcupine. They came to meet you."

"Fine, fine," said Brimhall, opening the door.

Raccoon and Porcupine came in.
"Any friend of Bear's is a
friend of mine," said Brimhall,
shaking their paws. "How nice
you happened to come just now.
I am about to fix a special meal
—the recipe is from Hawaii. It
has thirteen secret ingredients!"

"Imagine that!" said Raccoon.

"I can't wait!" said Porcupine.

"This better be good," said
Bear. "I made stew for dinner."

"We will have stew tomorrow,
Bear," said Brimhall. "Now, you
three visit while I fix dinner."

"What a fine fellow," Raccoon
whispered to Bear.

"His dinner smells very tasty,"
added Porcupine.

"Time to eat!" called Brimhall.
The table was set with Bear's
best dishes.
Two candles were burning bright.

"My, this is good," said Raccoon.

"Delicious!" added Porcupine.

"It was very nice of you,
Brimhall," murmured Bear.

Brimhall cleared the table and
served kumquats for dessert.
After dessert, Raccoon and
Porcupine thanked Brimhall and
Bear, and said good-bye.

"Er—Brimhall," said Bear, when their friends had gone, "you don't mind, then, about the mothballs—and the plants?"

"Why no, Bear," said Brimhall, "plants are only a hobby. You are more important. You are family. Anyway, I have decided to start a new hobby. A class meets on Tuesdays at Two Pines. It is called 'Painting in Oils.' "

"That sounds like a fine hobby, Brimhall," said Bear. "I'll just wash up these dishes now. You go sit in the living room."

Brimhall sat on the sofa, and
took a folder from his pocket.
"Paint on any surface," he read.
"Colorful flowers, fruit, trees..."
Brimhall looked at Bear's walls.
He looked at the shiny floors.
He looked up at the ceiling.

"Paint on dishes, glassware,
wood," he read on.
Brimhall watched Bear putting
dishes in the hall cupboard.
He glanced out the door at Bear's
plain wooden mailbox.
After a while, he put the folder
back in his pocket and dozed.
"There!" said Bear, coming into
the room. "The dishes are
washed and put away, and you've
had a nice nap. Do you feel
like a game of chess, Brimhall?"

"Fine!" said Brimhall, setting up the chessboard.

"It's good to have you here," said Bear. "You are a fine chess partner. The spare bedroom is just right for you. And it's far easier to cook for two, you know!"

JUDY DELTON is the author of *Two Good Friends* (an ALA Notable Book in 1974), *Rabbit Finds a Way, Two Is Company, Three Friends Find Spring*, and *Penny-Wise, Fun-Foolish*, among other books. She lives in Wisconsin with her four teen- and near-teen-age children. Brimhall came to stay in the Delton household some time ago, and Ms. Delton has been wanting to get him on paper ever since.

CYNDY SZEKERES is a noted illustrator and author/illustrator of children's books, whose work will be familiar to readers of *Cricket* magazine. She lives among various plants and animals in Vermont.

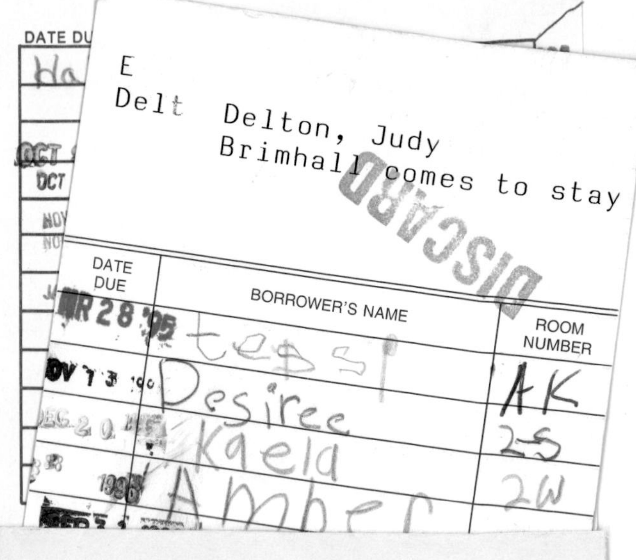
E
DEL Delton, Judy
Brimhall comes to stay
DATE DU
E
Delt Delton, Judy
Brimhall comes to stay
DISCARD
DATE DUE
BORROWER'S NAME
ROOM NUMBER
Desiree
AK
Kaela
2S
Amber
2W